Tweety's

KNOCK, KNOCK JOKES

Illustrated by Steve Smallwood

A GOLDEN BOOK • NEW YORK

Western Publishing Company, Inc., Racine, Wisconsin 53404

Tweety: Knock, knock.

Sylvester: Who's there?

Tweety: Gladys.

Sylvester: Gladys who?

Tweety: Gladys you and not that awful puddy tat!

Taz: Knock, knock.

Cooties: Who's there?

Taz: Iguana.

Cooties: Iguana who?

Taz: Iguana eat you for dinner.

Yosemite Sam: Knock, knock.

Bugs: Who's there?

Yosemite Sam: Europe.

Bugs: Europe who?

Yosemite Sam: Europe a creek without a paddle, varmint!

Daffy: Knock, knock.

Porky: Who's there?

Daffy: Vicious.

Porky: V-V-Vicious who?

Daffy: Vicious a Merry Christmas! (And a Happy New Year!)

Tweety: Knock, knock.

Sylvester: Who's there?

Tweety: Mandy.

Sylvester: Mandy who?

Tweety: Mandy lifeboats, the ship is sinking.

Speedy Gonzales: Knock, knock.

Daffy: Who's there?

Speedy Gonzales: Doris.

Daffy: Doris who?

Speedy Gonzales: Doris closed. That's why I'm knocking, señor!

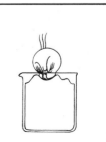

Miss Prissy: Knock, knock.

Foghorn Leghorn: Who's there?

Miss Prissy: Thumb.

Foghorn Leghorn: Thumb who?

Miss Prissy: Thumb day my prince will come . . .

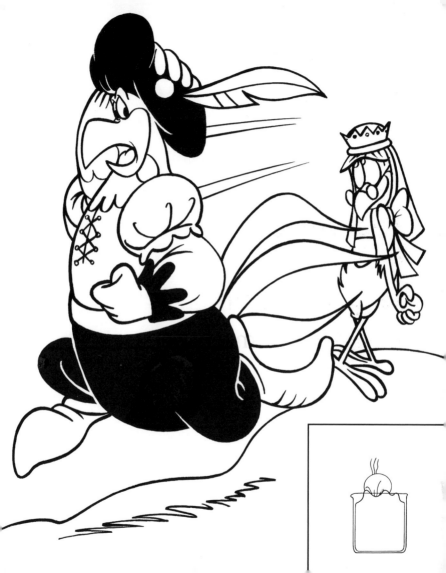

Petunia: Knock, knock.

Porky: Who's there?

Petunia: Shelby.

Porky: Sh-Sh-Shelby who?

Petunia: Shelby coming round the mountain when she comes!

Elmer: Knock, knock.

Bugs: Who's there?

Elmer: Luke.

Bugs: Luke who?

Elmer: Luke into my eyes! You're getting vewy sweepy.

Yosemite Sam: Knock, knock.

Bugs: Who's there?

Yosemite Sam: Yukon.

Bugs: Yukon who?

Yosemite Sam: Yukon say that again, varmint!

Tweety: Knock, knock.

Sylvester: Who's there?

Tweety: Hugo.

Sylvester: Hugo who?

Tweety: Hugo first, puddy tat. I'll wait here.

Daffy: Knock, knock.

Porky: Who's there?

Daffy: Midas.

Porky: M-M-Midas who?

Daffy: Midas well open the door and let me in!

Marvin the Martian: Knock, knock.

Duck Dodgers: Who's there?

Marvin the Martian: Atomic.

Duck Dodgers: Atomic who?

Marvin the Martian: Atomic ache! I have atomic ache. I ate too many Martian Meatballs.

Bugs: Knock, knock.

Yosemite Sam: Who's there?

Bugs: Robin.

Yosemite Sam: Robin who?

Bugs: Robin a coffin is dangerous. You could get into grave trouble!

Sylvester: Knock, knock.

Tweety: Who's there?

Sylvester: Ima.

Tweety: Ima who?

Sylvester: Ima zapped cat!

She-Devil: Knock, knock.

Taz: Who there?

She-Devil: Carrie.

Taz: Carrie who?

She-Devil: Carrie me, you big strong devil you!

Speedy Gonzales: Knock, knock.

Sylvester: Who's there?

Speedy Gonzales: Pecan.

Sylvester: Pecan who?

Speedy Gonzales: Pecan somebody your own size!

Porky: Knock, knock.

Daffy: Who's there?

Porky: W-W-Watson.

Daffy: Watson who?

Porky: W-W-Watson TV tonight? (Looney Tunes, I hope!)

Rocky: Knock, knock.

Mugsy: Who's there?

Rocky: Dwayne.

Mugsy: Dwayne who?

Rocky: Dwayne the bathtub, stupid! I'm drowning!

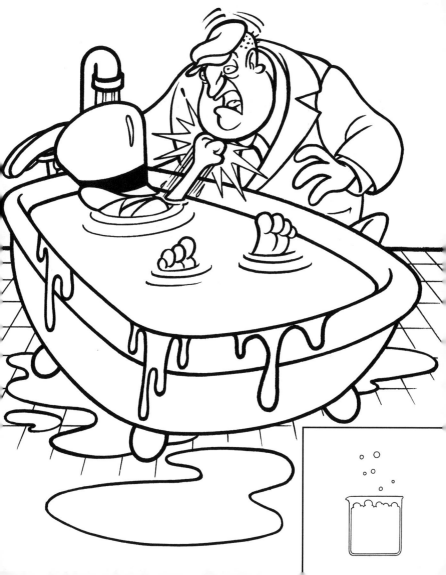

Tweety: Knock, knock.

Sylvester: Who's there?

Tweety: Olive.

Sylvester: Olive who?

Tweety: Olive a lot longer if you stop trying to eat me!

Granny: Knock, knock.

Tweety: Who's there?

Granny: Juicy.

Tweety: Juicy who?

Granny: Juicy Sylvester hiding anywhere?

Porky: Knock, knock.

Daffy: Who's there?

Porky: W-W-Weasel.

Daffy: Weasel who?

Porky: W-W-Weasel while you work.

Bugs: Knock, knock.

Elmer: Who's there?

Bugs: Wanda.

Elmer: Wanda who?

Bugs: Wanda who's knocking at the door!

Charlie Dog: Knock, knock.

Porky: Who-who-who's there?

Charlie Dog: Howard.

Porky: Howard who?

Charlie Dog: Howard you like to be the proud owner of a loyal dog? I'm 50 percent pointer, 50 percent Labrador retriever, 50 percent Irish setter . . .

Sylvester: Knock, knock.

Tweety: Who's there?

Sylvester: Amanda.

Tweety: Amanda who?

Sylvester: Amanda fix the plumbing!

Yosemite Sam: Knock, knock.

Bugs: Who's there?

Yosemite Sam: Stan.

Bugs: Stan who?

Yosemite Sam: Stan back, varmint! I'm comin' through!

Daffy: Knock, knock.

Porky: Who-who-who's there?

Daffy: Ivan.

Porky: Ivan who?

Daffy: Ivan to suck your blood!

Petunia: Knock, knock.

Cicero: Who's there?

Petunia: Coleen.

Cicero: Coleen who?

Petunia: Coleen up your room. It's a mess.

Tweety: Knock, knock.

Sylvester Jr.: Who's there?

Tweety: Canoe.

Sylvester Jr.: Canoe who?

Tweety: Canoe help me escape from the bad puddy tat?

Sam Sheepdog: Knock, knock.

Ralph Wolf: Who's there?

Sam Sheepdog: Jess.

Ralph Wolf: Jess who?

Sam Sheepdog: Jess little old me!

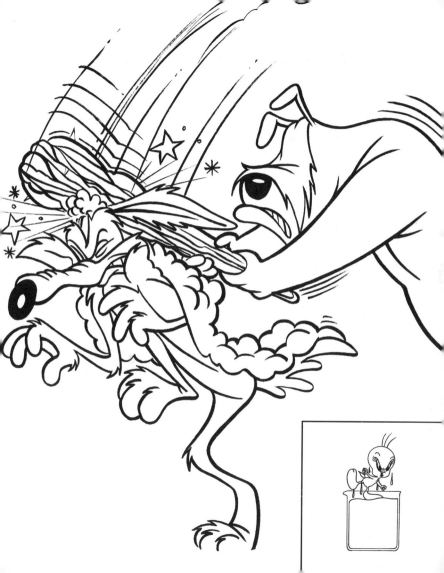

Bugs: Knock, knock.

Elmer: Who's there?

Bugs: Sadie.

Elmer: Sadie who?

Bugs: Sadie magic word and watch me disappear!

Daffy: Knock, knock.

Porky: Who-who-who's there?

Daffy: Ken.

Porky: Ken who?

Daffy: Ken you open the door? My foot's stuck in it!

Tweety: Knock, knock.

Sylvester: Who's there?

Tweety: Annapolis.

Sylvester: Annapolis who?

Tweety: Ann apol is good to eat!

Henery Hawk: Knock, knock.

Foghorn Leghorn: Who's there?

Henery Hawk: Butcher.

Foghorn Leghorn: Butcher who?

Henery Hawk: Butcher money where your mouth is, chicken!

Daffy: Knock, knock.

Daffy: Who's there?

Daffy: Yuri.

Daffy: Yuri who?

Daffy: Yuri big star, babe! You're the greatest! They love you!

Tweety: Knock, knock.

Sylvester: Who's there?

Tweety: Dwight.

Sylvester: Dwight who?

Tweety: Dwight stuff on your fur is only dandruff!

Witch Hazel: Knock, knock.

Bugs: Who's there?

Witch Hazel: Demons.

Bugs: Demons who?

Witch Hazel: Demons are a ghoul's best friend!

Daffy: Knock, knock.

Elmer: Who's there?

Daffy: Deduct.

Elmer: Deduct who?

Daffy: Deduct named Daffy, that's who!

Speedy Gonzales: Knock, knock.

Slowpoke Rodriguez: Who's there?

Speedy Gonzales: José.

Slowpoke Rodriguez: José who?

Speedy Gonzales: José can you see by the dawn's early light?

Tweety: Knock, knock.

Sylvester: Who's there?

Tweety: Wendy.

Sylvester: Wendy who?

Tweety: Wendy puddy tat's away, the bird will play!

Yosemite Sam: Knock, knock.

Bugs: Who's there?

Yosemite Sam: Itch.

Bugs: Itch who?

Yosemite Sam: Itch your mother, Bugs! Why haven't you called?

Chester: Knock, knock.

Spike: Who's there?

Chester: Howard.

Spike: Howard who?

Chester: Howard you like to go beat up on some cats, huh, Spike?

Tweety: Knock, knock.

Sylvester: Who's there?

Tweety: Ammonia.

Sylvester: Ammonia who?

Tweety: Ammonia little birdie!

Duck Dodgers: Knock, knock.

Marvin the Martian: Who's there?

Duck Dodgers: Razor.

Marvin the Martian: Razor who?

Duck Dodgers: Razor hands! I want that Aludium Q-36 Explosive Space Modulator!

Elmer Fudd: Knock, knock.

Bugs Bunny: Who's there?

Elmer Fudd: Wok.

Bugs Bunny: Wok who?

Elmer Fudd: Wok and woll is here to stay!

Porky: Knock, knock.

Elmer: Who's there?

Porky: A-A-Amos.

Elmer: Amos who?

Porky: A-A-Amosquito bit me!

Pepé Le Pew: Knock, knock.

Penelope: Who's there?

Pepé Le Pew: Z.

Penelope: Z who?

Pepé Le Pew: Z time for love is now, ma chérie!

Tweety:
Knock, knock.

Sylvester:
Who's there?

Tweety:
Shirley.

Sylvester:
Shirley who?

Tweety:
Shirley you don't expect me to come in, do you?